A CALDWELL CHRISTMAS

SUITOR'S CROSSING: THE CALDWELLS #6

HALLIE BENNETT

I0619349

Copyright © 2025 by Hallie Bennett

Wait!

Have you read the entire Caldwell series yet?

Read each sibling's steamy romance <u>here</u>[1] first!

PROLOGUE

DECEMBER 3

DONALD CALDWELL (GRAMPS)

The heat emanating from the electric fireplace warms my toes as Greta cuddles closer to me on the sofa.

Nothing beats the crackle of real flames and the smell of ash in the air, but I can't complain too much about the artificial fire. Not when my girl is snuggled into my side.

"Have you heard from Kennedy and Wyatt today?" Greta asks, her head tipping back to meet my eyes.

"Not yet. They're probably settling in after the long flight."

My granddaughter was surprised by her husband with a trip to Vienna in honor of their fifth anniversary. Wyatt has been planning the vacation for months—sorting out their travel and arranging for Soren and Diana to babysit their three-year-old son, Tristan. One of my adorable great-grandbabies.

Our family is full of little tykes these days.

Thinking about the changes in my grandchildren's lives over the past five years brings a smile to my face.

Kennedy used to be so shy.

Kept to herself.

Until a pen pal mishap with a soldier overseas.

Sherry still hasn't forgiven Kennedy—or the rest of the family—for how things went down back then, even though it was her son's fault for fumbling Kennedy in the first place. If he hadn't been such a jerk, there wouldn't have been an opening for his commanding officer to steal my granddaughter's heart.

"You're probably right." Greta sighs and settles her head back on my chest. "I can't believe they've been together for five years already. Time sure does fly."

"Especially when you're with the one you love," I say, pressing a kiss to her crown.

"Hopefully, Tristan isn't giving Soren and Diana too much trouble. I know Wyatt was wary of letting them babysit over Beth and Beckett. They've got a lot on their plate with Sara Beth and Rachel."

My eldest grandson certainly has a full life.

A few years ago, it was just Soren and his daughter, Sara Beth. But Sara Beth's bunny faked an injury, and one visit to the veterinarian later, Diana crashed into their lives.

She's loosened up my formerly grumpy grandson, and I couldn't be happier with the change in him. Or the little girl they added to their family—another great-grandchild to add to my roster of loved ones.

"They can handle it. Besides, it's easier for Soren to watch a toddler than Beckett. His schedule at the firehouse means Beth would be alone most of the time trying to wrangle the kid."

"Don't underestimate Beth." Greta pats my stomach in reproach.

Chuckling, I cover her hand with mine. "I'm not. I have all the faith in the world in that girl, but two is better than one. Plus, Soren and Diana have Sara Beth as backup."

"Sixteen years old. It was only yesterday that she was ten years old gushing about Whiskers."

"And now her focus is on friends and boys." There have been several times when her dad has ranted about the foibles of teenage boys as if he's forgotten he used to be one of them.

Though Soren was never as bad as Beckett.

He was the troublemaker of the group. As different as night and day from his twin, Ezra, and their youngest brother, Griffen.

Which reminds me...

"How was your call with Heidi earlier? She and Griff are still coming for Christmas, right?"

"Of course. They did a combination Thanksgiving and Christmas celebration with her parents, since the three of them will be spending the holiday in Suitor's Crossing rather than Guardian Valley."

Greta's excitement is palpable, energy vibrating through her body.

When Heidi first arrived in town, she started volunteering at the senior center, and almost immediately, Greta took her under her wing. It soon became obvious that Heidi was interested in my quiet grandson, which was when Greta and I cooked up a scheme to get the two together.

One that worked perfectly, considering they're married with a two-year-old girl named Joy, after Heidi's grandmother.

"It'll be good to have the entire family together again," I say, glancing out the window when a rogue branch cracks against the glass. Wind buffets the side of the apartment we share at Golden

Living, a senior community in Suitor's Crossing, and I can tell we're in for a cold December.

"Maybe we can have that magazine photographer take a family photo for us," Greta suggests. "Our last group shot is missing the twins."

Ezra and Lauren's twin babies weren't born yet, though she'd been heavily pregnant for the Christmas photo last year.

"I think family portraits are a little below a national magazine photographer's paygrade."

"Nonsense. He's here to document Ezra and Lauren's lives, and we're a part of it."

I know better than to argue with her logic, and hell, Greta has a way of getting what she wants. It wouldn't surprise me if she sweet-talked the photographer into a side project.

"Yes, dear," I tease, squeezing her closer. "One thing is for sure. This Christmas will be one to remember."

CHAPTER ONE

DECEMBER 6

BETH CALDWELL

Glittery candy canes catch my eye the moment Diana, Lauren, and I enter a local boutique. Red and white sparkles on the tiny onesie, begging my fingers to trace the cuteness overload.

"Ugh, I miss my babies being that size," Lauren says from my right. She strokes the soft cotton without hesitation.

"I know. Rachel is growing too fast—a toddler going on twelve."

We laugh at Diana's description. Thanks to her older sister, Rachel definitely has a lot of sass, or maybe that's just part of being in the middle of the 'terrible twos.'

Lauren and Diana lament their children's latest growth spurts as they move deeper into the store in search of holiday gifts, but I linger by the onesie, contemplating my doctor's appointment this morning.

I'd scheduled it after several bouts of nausea before breakfast and checking the calendar for when my last period ended. While

Beckett and I weren't actively trying to get pregnant, we weren't *not* trying. We don't use condoms, and my birth control has been gathering dust in a bathroom drawer for months.

Our philosophy is if it happens, it happens.

And surprise! A baby is on the way.

"Beth, are you okay?" Diana calls from the back of the store.

"Yep, just zoned out for a second," I joke, hurrying to join my sisters-in-law. I'm dying to share my secret, but no one can know before Beckett.

And unfortunately, this isn't something I can text. It needs to be in-person. Preferably in a quirky manner like videos I've seen.

Good thing he's at the firehouse for the next forty-eight hours, so I'll have time to think.

And freak out.

I don't always love my husband's schedule. The long hours that include several nights where we're forced to sleep apart. It took some getting used to in the beginning, and now I'll need to readjust again because we'll have a baby.

One where I won't have help for extended stretches of time.

Nerves gather in my belly as I self-consciously place my hand over what will soon be a prominent bump.

"What do you think of this for Ezra?" Lauren holds up an insulated coffee mug with *DAD* engraved on the front. "They offer etching services, so I can add Nash and Ryan's names in cursive to match the display."

I study the sample mug on the shelf and agree that it's cute.

Maybe I should get Beckett one of the mugs that says World's Best Dad *to break the news of his impending fatherhood...*

CHAPTER TWO

LAUREN CALDWELL

S omething is going on with Beth. She's unusually quiet, and that's saying something since she's the most introverted out of the three of us.

But ever since Diana and I picked her up at her place for this holiday shopping trip, she's been off in her own world.

"I like it," Diana says, grabbing another *DAD* mug from the shelf. "I can get one for Soren with Sara Beth and Rachel's names. Then they can match. I'll text Kennedy and Heidi to see if they want us to buy them for Wyatt and Griffen, too."

Beth tentatively selects a navy one. "If it's a family affair, Beckett should have one. Don't want the shop to run out by the time he needs it." A red blush blooms on her cheeks as she ducks her head.

Diana and I share a speculative look, unaware that Beckett and Beth were thinking of having kids soon.

"Sounds like a plan. Let's—" The blare of an incoming call rings from my phone, and I quickly remove it from my coat pocket to silence the noise. "Crap! It's the magazine; I should take this."

"Go ahead. We'll keep browsing." Beth smiles and shoos me away.

Returning the mug to its place temporarily, I exit the boutique and shiver at the icy blast that hits me in the face.

"Hello?"

"Mrs. Caldwell? This is Jeannie from Q Magazine confirming the arrival of our photographer and journalist on December 11. They will be staying at Hearthstone Lodge through December 14. Does that still work for you and your husband?"

Why Ezra and I agreed to an introspective look into our lives, I'll never know. It's not like we need the publicity. The lodge has never been busier with guests booked out over a year in advance, and my songwriting talents are clamored for by today's top musical artists.

But Ezra's PR person and my agent talked us into it.

A holiday special on the life and love between a billionaire and his famous songwriting wife, who also happened to be in the middle of a reality TV scandal years ago.

"Yes, those dates work for us. We're looking forward to meeting the team."

Because the sooner they get here, the sooner this interview will be done and I can focus on what's really stressing me out: hosting our family's Christmas at the house we just finished building.

It's the only one large enough to host six couples and their children for the holiday, which is exactly what Ezra and I wanted when we planned the home—for it to be a place of gathering for the Caldwell clan—but the reality is a lot more stressful than I was expecting.

Oh, how naive you were, Lauren.

"Excellent. Thank you for confirming, and happy holidays." The lady hangs up, and I take a deep breath.

"You've got this," I say to myself.

And if not?

Well, the Caldwells thrive in chaos, right?

CHAPTER THREE

DECEMBER 13

EZRA CALDWELL

"Like mama, like son, huh?" I stare down at the splat of orange goop Nash spit on my white button-down shirt. The squash mixture isn't as cold as the iced coffee Lauren accidentally dumped on me years ago, but I definitely have to change my top before our last session with the Q Magazine photographer.

"Sara Beth, would you mind watching Nash and Ryan while I change?"

My niece jerks her head away from the crew adding finishing touches to the set—or what used to be Hearthstone Lodge's main lobby. After yesterday's *Day in the Life* focus at our new home, today is an homage to the family legacy which brought Lauren and I together, complete with a giant Christmas tree and a blazing fireplace decked with garland and stockings.

"Sure... I think Lauren is still upstairs getting ready, too." Sara Beth takes my seat in front of the twins to continue feeding them their lunch.

Technically, she's here to provide extra baby monitoring while Lauren and I talk with the Q Magazine journalist, but a behind-the-scenes look into what goes into a major magazine spread captured her attention from day one.

And Lauren and I haven't wanted to quell that curiosity by forcing her to do more with the kids.

Now, though, it's necessary.

Glancing at my watch, I calculate how much time we have before the lunch break is over. "We've got about twenty more minutes before things pick up again. Lauren and I will be back by then."

"No worries. I've got this," Sara Beth says with a grin, airplaning a tiny spoon into Ryan's open mouth.

Satisfied that my children are in good hands, I hurry to the bank of elevators and head to the executive suite.

Voices sound from the living area the moment I step inside. Lauren is curled on an overstuffed chair in front of a view of the mountains, a terrycloth robe wrapped around her generous curves.

"It reminded me of that Hallmark movie you liked so much. The one with the musician in Vienna with Calder Mayfield as the lead."

I recognize my sister, Kennedy's, voice bursting through the speakerphone.

My brother-in-law, Wyatt, surprised her with an anniversary trip to Vienna to explore their holiday market, and it's clear by her excitement that she's loving every second of their vacation.

"It's too bad you're not there while they're filming a movie. How cool would it be to actually meet one of the stars?" Lauren titters. "I'd totally fawn over Thatcher North."

I frown at the admiration in her tone. My wife should only have eyes for me, not some Hollywood actor. Leaning over the back of the chair, my palm tips her chin up for a swift kiss.

"Forget North," I grumble, "Your husband requires all your attention."

Kennedy laughs in the background as Lauren smirks. "Jealous much?"

"Always when it comes to you."

Lauren shakes her head at my Neanderthal ways, something that only seemed to emerge once I met her. "You're ridiculous. You know you're the only man for me."

"Besides, just because we're married, that doesn't mean we can't look. We're not dead," Kennedy pipes up.

Wyatt's answering growl is immediately cut short as the video call ends. Guess my brother-in-law agrees with me when it comes to our women and their famous crushes.

"You're ridiculous," Lauren says with a half-grin before sighing, her features dimming a bit.

"What's wrong? I'm only joking about North."

"It's not that." She waves a hand and moves towards the dress hanging on the back of the bathroom door.

"What is it then?" I ask.

"Just thinking about everything I have to do before Christmas. I'm glad we only have a few hours left with the Q Magazine people. Then, I can focus."

"Babe, you don't need to stress about Christmas."

"Of course, I do," she says. "It's our first holiday in the new house and your entire family will be here. Heidi and Griffen are traveling from Montana. Wyatt and Kennedy will be back from Europe. It'll be a full house, and I want everything to be perfect."

"When has anything in our family ever been perfect? You know we can be a messy bunch."

Lauren shrugs.

I know my wife well enough to know she doesn't believe me.

Snagging the back of her robe, I tug until she bumps into my chest, and I can wrap my arms around her waist.

"Why don't I offer a little stress relief?"

"Ezra..." she drawls, amusement tinging her voice. "We shouldn't."

Fuck that.

"We definitely should. Think of it as interview prep. My girl needs to be relaxed and happy before meeting with the journalist."

Her hand inches upward to cup my cheek as she tilts her head back. "Well, when you put it that way..."

I chuckle and drop a soft kiss to her lips.

My fingers slip below the edge of her robe to cup her breast, teasing one of her nipples with my thumb. The swollen bud is extra sensitive these days, since she's still breastfeeding, and it doesn't take much before Lauren whimpers, begging for more.

My other hand slides between her thighs to part the slick folds of her sex.

"Forget about family dinners and magazine interviews. Focus on me. On this. Focus on the feel of my fingers sliding into this hot pussy." I mimic my words, groaning at the tight clasp of her soaking slit.

"Does that feel good, baby?"

"You know it does," she pants.

My thumb circles her clit as I keep up a steady, thrusting rhythm, while playing with her nipples.

I lick and suck the sweet skin beneath my mouth. Adding little love bites along her jaw and neck.

The makeup artist downstairs will have a fun time covering up my marks, I'm sure.

Lauren's plush ass cradles my hard cock, but I ignore my own need.

This isn't about me.

It's about her.

I don't want Lauren stressing about Christmas. I'll hire whoever I need to help her, but I know she wants to do this herself, which I admire even as her stubbornness concerns me.

"Ezra!" Lauren gasps and arches in my arms. Her orgasm vibrates through her body before she slumps into me.

Carefully removing my fingers and licking them clean, I hike her into my arms and carry her to the bed.

"No, wait... I have to get dressed," she mumbles.

"You can rest for a couple of minutes. We're the stars of the show. They can wait."

"It's rude to be late."

"I'll take full responsibility for our rudeness," I joke.

"Love you," she murmurs, her eyes fluttering shut.

"I love you, too, baby."

More than words could ever fully express.

CHAPTER FOUR

DECEMBER 17

HEIDI CALDWELL

Joy continues crying as we disembark from the plane. She did not like her first flight—no matter how many cuddles, toys, and snacks we offered her—and now, Griffen is talking about driving back home after Christmas.

Like a nine-hour drive is better than a two-hour flight.

"You'd think she would have tired herself out already," I say, rubbing circles over Joy's back while Griffen grabs our checked baggage.

"Toddler stamina is no joke."

He swings our two extra-large luggage carriers off the metal carousel, and we follow the crowd of travelers heading toward the Arrivals sign and a parking garage.

Soren offered to pick us up, and as soon as we exit the airport, his huge truck comes into view.

"Good to see you, brother." Griffen and Soren hug before he turns to Joy and me. "Someone's having a rough day, huh?"

"Hopefully, she'll calm down on the ride to Suitor's Crossing." I mentally cross my fingers, and thankfully, once we're on the highway, she falls asleep, so the only sound in the truck cab is softly playing Christmas music on the radio.

Relaxing in the front passenger seat, I stare out the window. A forest of trees lines the road as we near the mountains. Snow blankets the highest ridges in a picturesque display, and a part of me misses living here full time.

Montana is gorgeous with its own big sky and mountain views, but I always feel nostalgic when Griffen and I visit Suitor's Crossing.

This is where we fell in love.

This is where Joy was born.

It was the beginning of our love story, so it'll always hold a special place in my heart.

When we arrive at Hearthstone Lodge, a staff member collects our luggage and leads us to a prepared suite on the top floor. Soren had a trail ride to prepare for, but Ezra and Lauren are waiting for us once we step outside the elevator.

"There's my favorite little brother!" Ezra grins and slaps Griffen on the back before going in for a hug.

"Technically, I'm your only little brother."

"Semantics. How was the flight?" The guys launch into a conversation about crowded airports and inefficient systems, while Lauren and I move to the bedroom.

"She's so sweet," Lauren coos, lightly brushing a finger over the back of Joy's clenched fist. "Are you trying to give me baby fever?"

I laugh at the gleam in her eyes. "You're still breastfeeding your one-year-olds. Surely, you're not ready for more yet."

She rolls her eyes toward the ceiling and sighs. "You're right, but a girl would be nice. Imagine how cute it would be to have Nash and Ryan as her protective older brothers."

"I don't have to imagine it; I've heard Kennedy bemoan her brothers' antics enough times to know what the poor girl would have to endure."

"You've got a point there. And Ezra would be a grumpy Papa Bear."

"That's not much of a leap. He's the grump of the twins already," I say, carefully laying Joy on the bed and nudging pillows against her sides to keep her from rolling.

"But he's better than he used to be."

"Thanks to you." I grin. The Caldwells love to share how Lauren made their by-the-book brother break the rules. Like punching a guy in a grocery store after he insulted Lauren.

She helped him loosen up.

"Don't act like you haven't brought Griffen out of his shell."

"True... But I doubt that openness will extend to anyone interested in our daughter when the time comes." An image of Griffen with a frown on his face comes to mind as I study Joy's adorable sleeping face. "Poor girl will have quite the time dating when she's older."

"Who's dating?" Griffen asks as he and Ezra enter the room.

Lauren and I share a look before I say, "Joy."

"Don't even go there, Heidi. Soren's shared all the trouble he's having with Sara Beth now that she's sixteen. Did you know that some boy from chemistry class asked her to the winter formal?"

"I did." Diana had messaged the group chat between all the sisters after Sara Beth dropped the bomb on her parents.

The overprotective bluster from the Caldwell men is sweet and hilarious—a preview into my daughter's future. Patting Griffen's broad shoulder, I try to reassure him.

"Sara Beth can handle herself, just like our daughter will when the time comes."

"I hope that time never comes. She can become a nun."

"Oh my god... You did not just say that."

The four of us devolve into the merits of convents and laughter over the ridiculousness of the topic.

And I wouldn't have life any other way than filled with family—even if they are a little crazy.

CHAPTER FIVE

DECEMBER 19

SOREN CALDWELL

I pace in front of the living room's bay window while Rachel and Tristan play with a herd of horses Rachel got for her third birthday.

"Look, Daddy!" She holds a black and white horse over her head to show off the sparkly pink butterflies in its mane and tail. Apparently, the green ones weren't good enough judging by their scattered presence on the area rug.

"Good job, baby," I say with a faint smile.

Rather than on the daughter at my feet, my mind is on my eldest upstairs. The sixteen-year-old going on her first date tonight.

Diana has spent the past two hours up there helping Sara Beth get ready, while I watch Rachel and try not to freak out about my girl attending winter formal with a boy instead of her friends.

"Look at mine!" My nephew waves a chestnut pony in the air. It has a glittery halter and saddle hooked around its plastic body while its wild hair remains free of adornment.

When my sister's husband shared his plans to whisk Kennedy away to Vienna for an anniversary trip, I immediately volunteered to watch Tristan for them. The same age as my daughter, I figured the two rugrats would have fun together, and it would be easier for me to babysit than Ezra with his one-year-old twins.

"Nice buddy. Maybe this weekend we can visit the stables, and I can show you how to put a halter and saddle on a real horse."

"Cool!" Tristan and Rachel high-five as she squeals in excitement. She loves hanging out at the lodge with me.

Another generation of Caldwells to continue our family's legacy at the lodge, even though Tristan is technically a Lincoln. But we consider Wyatt an honorary Caldwell.

Diana sweeps into the room, an air of anticipation riding in her wake. "Sara Beth looks beautiful." She bends to pick up Rachel and faces the bottom of the staircase. "Are you ready to see her?"

"Yeah!" Rachel and Tristan cry simultaneously.

I give a less enthusiastic nod.

"Alright, come on down."

The swish of fabric brushing across the floor precedes the tip-tap of heels on the hardwood stairs.

The kids gasp as Sara Beth practically floats down the steps in a sea of silver silk and organza. Her hair is braided into a crown on her head that holds a few sprigs of white holiday berries.

"You look like a princess!" Rachel shouts, clasping her hands over her heart in awe.

Sara Beth spins in a circle to cause her skirt to flare. She really does look like a princess.

There's a pain in my chest.

My girl is growing up.

"You're gorgeous, baby."

"Thanks, Dad," she says with a blush. The doorbell rings, and her eyes widen.

That must be Joseph.

Diana pulls out her phone to check the time and nods. "Punctual. We like that in a guy, don't we?" She elbows me in the side, and I grunt in response.

Diana laughs, knowing my feelings about Sara Beth going on a date with Joseph Benson.

He seems like a good kid, but Sara Beth is still my baby girl.

I open the door with a grimace. Although, maybe it's closer to a glare based on the way Joseph looks like he's about to piss his pants.

"Hello, Mr. Caldwell. I'm here to pick up Sara Beth."

"Dad, move. Let him in."

I reluctantly step to the side.

"Picture time," Diana cries, scooting the kids closer for a ton of photos before pushing me in for one with Sara Beth.

"Remember your curfew," I warn once we're done. "Eleven o'clock. Sharp."

"We've got it, Dad." Sara Beth groans, tugging on Joseph's arm.

"And if you need anything, just call," I say, watching as they trek down the porch, the sidewalk, the drive, until reaching Joseph's car parked on the curb.

"They'll be fine. You've raised a good girl," Diana murmurs, wrapping an arm around me.

"I'm a good girl!" Rachel shouts from her place in my wife's other arm.

"Yes, you are." I lean over to tickle her.

"Hey, what about me?" Tristan calls, still in the living room with the horses.

"You're a good girl, too," I tease.

"I'm a boy."

"Oh, how could I forget?" I grab his waist and haul him in the air. "I think your mom and dad are planning to call tonight to say hello. Are you excited?"

"I'm going to show them my horse."

"Excellent plan. I'm sure they'll love it."

After setting Rachel down so she can rejoin her cousin playing, Diana curls her arms around my waist again and rests her chin on my chest.

"How are you really doing?"

"Wishing my little girl wasn't so grown up," I admit.

"Look on the bright side. You still have another girl to go through the same growing pains with."

"Don't remind me... Rachel, you're never going to grow up on Daddy, are you?" I ask.

"Never grow up?" Her nose wrinkles. "Like Peter Pan?"

She doesn't like that idea.

But, of course, her favorite movies don't involve flying boys and pirates. She is more into talking animals at this point.

"I know this is sad," Diana says. "But it's a good thing. Our kids are becoming independent."

"I know, I know," I agree.

Diana smiles, then stands on her tiptoes to press a kiss to my lips. Before she can retreat, I hold her there, cupping her cheeks with my palms. Needing those extra seconds of comfort from my wife.

"I love you," I whisper.

And I always will.

CHAPTER SIX

DECEMBER 21

KENNEDY LINCOLN (NÉE CALDWELL)

The scent of lavender floats in the air, a marked contrast from the cinnamon that has been surrounding me from the moment Wyatt and I arrived in Austria. Wandering through the hotel suite, I find my husband in the bathroom kneeling beside the bathtub.

"What are you doing?" I ask, although it's obvious with the water filling the white porcelain.

"Drawing you a bath. You pushed too hard today."

I roll my eyes at his soft reprimand, though secretly I'm pleased he cares so much.

And he's not wrong.

We spent the day walking around Vienna, exploring the holiday market and a few touristy attractions. I've never had so many steps accounted for on my tracker than this trip, and today has been the highest yet.

Something my back and feet definitely don't appreciate.

"We took breaks," I argue.

"Not enough of them," Wyatt counters with a dark brow raised.

I sigh. "Not enough of them."

With my spina bifida and scoliosis, chronic back pain is a way of life, but I could have done better at preventing more pain than usual by pacing myself today.

Though it's hard because I want to get in as much as I can before Wyatt and I head back to Suitor's Crossing for Christmas.

"If we don't get to everything this round, we can come back with Tristan in tow."

"Are you secretly a mind reader?" I tease. "I was just thinking about not wanting to miss anything on this trip."

"No mindreading. I just know *you*." He dries off his hands after testing the heat of the water and stands. "Everything is ready for you now."

"Will you be joining me?" I ask as I slip out of my clothes. Wool socks. Fleece-lined leggings. *Cozy warmth* is the theme of my wardrobe for this trip.

"If you'll have me." He grins and reaches for the buttons on his shirt as I nod. Wyatt steps into the tub first, then carefully guides me down so my back rests against his chest.

After a few minutes of quiet and letting the heat of the water soak in, I let out a heavy breath. "I miss Tristan."

Our three-year-old son is enjoying an extended play date with his cousin Rachel, and while I appreciate a romantic couples-only getaway, this is the longest I've been away from him since he was born.

"Me too. But he's fine. Soren and Diana are taking good care of him." Wyatt soaps up his hands before massaging my shoulders, slowly working his way down my aching muscles.

"I know..." He kneads a particularly sore spot, and I moan. "I swear you get better at that every time."

"I probably do. Practice makes perfect, after all."

I hum in my throat in agreement, allowing my mind to drift. "Though you didn't need that much practice, did you? Remember the first time you gave me a back massage?"

"The day we officially met," he says. I can hear the smile in his voice.

"Yep, and it was pretty relaxing then, too... Considering you were practically a stranger." I laugh.

"A stranger in love with you."

"Thanks to Sherry."

"Oh, god, Sherry. She still glares at me any time our paths cross in town."

"At least she acknowledges you." I lightly splash water on his exposed knee. "She always turns the other way or pretends I don't exist whenever we bump into each other."

"You'd think she'd be over what happened between you and Chris considering he's engaged to someone else now."

"No one holds a grudge like Sherry," I say breathlessly, distracted by Wyatt's hard cock sliding between my ass cheeks. I squirm in his lap, causing the water to splash against the sides of the tub.

"Is my girl thinking naughty thoughts?" he growls.

"Maybe..."

His roughened palms glide upward to hold my breasts. His thumbs tweak the nipples. "You shouldn't be exerting yourself."

Reaching back, I brace a hand on the back of his head and rock against his firm body.

"Well, I've got a husband, haven't I? Perhaps he can do all the work."

"Hmm... Maybe he can." One of his hands dips below the water and slips between my parted thighs. "You sexy little tease. This bath was meant to relax you, not act as foreplay."

"I find orgasms very relaxing," I taunt.

He releases my breast long enough to guide my mouth to his for a scorching kiss, and I moan at the possessive parry and thrust of his tongue.

Blunt-tipped fingers dive into my pussy, and I clench around the thick digits before he replaces his fingers with his cock. Wyatt swallows my gasp.

"Hang on, pretty girl." He uses his knees to spread my legs wider, and more water gushes over the porcelain lip onto the tile. We're making a mess. A wet, slippery mess.

And I've never felt more alive.

The lights of Vienna create a colorful glow through the tall windows. Lavender and Wyatt's spicy cologne tickle my nose. And with each powerful thrust of his cock, a bond of love and pleasure tangle together—never to be broken.

CHAPTER SEVEN

DECEMBER 24

WYATT LINCOLN

I knock on the cabin door, and a burst of activity erupts behind the thick wood before Soren swings it open with a harried expression on his face.

"Daddy!" Tristan sneaks around his uncle's legs to wrap his arms around mine. His chin bumps my knee as he tilts his head back to shoot a beaming grin up at me—one that burns a hole through my heart.

God, I love this kid.

Reaching down, I lift him in my arms for a hug while Kennedy rounds my side to kiss his cheek.

"How's my big boy? Were you good for Uncle Soren and Aunt Diana?" she asks, tickling his belly and eliciting a squeal of happiness.

"Uh-huh. Rachel and I played horses, and Sara Beth was a princess." His *r*'s sound more like *w*'s, but I've missed the ramblings of my son.

Exploring Vienna with Kennedy filled my soul with more joy than I ever fathomed as she lit up at each new discovery, but there was a noticeable Tristan-shaped absence.

"I know! Your aunt sent us pictures."

Soren motions us inside the warm cabin where Rachel is coloring at the dining table, Sara Beth is on her phone, and Diana flits around the kitchen. It smells like Christmas heaven, and my stomach grumbles, eager for our family's Christmas Eve feast back at home.

While the entire Caldwell clan will gather tomorrow at Ezra and Lauren's new home for a huge holiday dinner, tonight is all about the individual sibling families. A little time alone to strengthen those core bonds before converging into one giant group.

Kennedy bends over the back of Sara Beth's chair to hug her from behind. "You looked gorgeous. How was the dance?"

"Good. The snowflake decorations turned out great with all the twinkling lights." She'd been part of the decorating committee for the winter formal, so I'm not surprised that's her first comment.

"And Joseph?" Kennedy's brows wiggle comically while her brother groans.

"He got her back before curfew, so there's that," he says.

Sara Beth rolls her eyes. "Joseph was fun. He made sure I never got thirsty and let me borrow his jacket on the drive home."

"Aww... That's sweet."

"Right? That's what I said." Diana sets a bowl of rolls on the table before pulling my wife in for a hug. "How do you feel being back in Suitor's Crossing? Missing your European tour yet?"

Kennedy laughs. "An abbreviated tour. We didn't even venture into one of the surrounding countries because there was so much to see where we were."

She launches into an update of the last few days of our trip while I settle on the living room couch. Tristan wiggles out of my arms to join Rachel coloring.

"Abandoning me already? I've been gone for weeks."

"You can't compete with *My Little Pony*. He's a *Bro-ny* now," Soren jokes, watching the kids with fondness.

Catching Kennedy's eye, she raises two fingers, and I nod, understanding the quiet communication. We don't want to spend all evening hijacking Soren and his family's Christmas.

"Want to know what *does* compete?" I question, determined to capture my son's attention again, rather than a herd of fictional horses that need coloring. "Christmas presents."

"Presents?" Both toddlers look up with an avaricious gleam in their eyes.

Soren groans and rubs the back of his neck. "Now you've done it."

"Yep," I say, standing and heading toward the front door, knowing Kennedy won't be too far behind with her two-minute warning earlier. "We've got to get home for dinner, and if you're good, you'll get to choose which present you want to open for Christmas Eve. Unless you want to stay here and color..."

"No!" Tristan jumps to his feet and races around the cabin giving everyone hurried hugs while Kennedy and I chuckle at his enthusiasm. "Bye-bye! Love you! Let's go, Daddy!"

"Demanding little tyke, isn't he?" Diana sweeps a hand over his head while Rachel hops around her feet begging to open a present, too.

"Like mother, like son." I wink and Kennedy blushes.

"Ugh... I did not need to hear that." Soren gently pushes us out the door. "And thanks for getting Rach riled up about presents." His voice lowers. "Payback's gonna be a bitch."

I grin then get my family tucked safely into my truck. We carefully descend the mountain Soren's cabin sits on, but before I can make the turn towards our own house, Kennedy taps my arm and points in the opposite direction.

"How about a detour? King Bishop's Holiday Lane display isn't too far away, and I've got some cookies we can enjoy while checking out the lights."

"Yay, cookies!" Tristan shouts, his fists rising in the air from his car seat.

"Cookies before dinner? My girl is such a rebel," I tease as I flick the blinker to go left rather than right.

"You know it. Otherwise, I never would have picked up with you after that first letter."

"Naughty girl," I whisper. "Writing one man when you were supposed to be writing another."

"Oh, the scandal." Kennedy dramatically places her hand over her heart. "Suitor's Crossing will never be the same."

"Sherry will never be the same," I correct, claiming her hand in mine and resting it on my thigh.

The truth is *I* was never the same man after the first time Kennedy wrote Sherry's son, Chris.

A lonely, deployed soldier, I didn't get letters from home like the other men in my unit. When Chris received that initial message, then promptly tossed it, my life forever changed.

Thanks to his thoughtlessness, I have a wife I love—my *heart spark* as Suitor's Crossing locals would call her—and a son I adore. Not to mention the extended family of siblings who treat me like one of their own.

Kennedy gave me everything I never dared hope for but am damn grateful to have.

CHAPTER EIGHT

DECEMBER 24

DIANA CALDWELL

Once Wyatt, Kennedy, and Tristan leave, I return to the kitchen to finish preparing for tonight's Christmas Eve dinner. I appreciate this tradition we started a few years ago once all the Caldwell siblings were coupled up and having children.

As much as I look forward to tomorrow, when everyone will get together, I love having an evening to celebrate the holiday with my husband and kids.

"Hey, baby." Soren eases behind me and rests his hands on my hips. "Everything smells great. Do you need any help?"

"Can you finish the salad, please?" Raising my voice, I turn toward Sara Beth. "Sara, do you mind wrangling your sister into her booster seat?"

"Got it." She shoves her phone into her pocket then heads to the living room to scoop Rachel into her arms. My three-year-old giggles and pretends to fly like Santa's reindeer.

It's crazy how different life looks these days. I moved to Suitor's Crossing for change a little over five years ago, and it more than delivered.

From my handsome husband to my two rambunctious girls, taking the leap of faith to quit my old job and come here has been well worth it.

The four of us sit around the dining table, passing food bowls, and chatting about Rachel's latest obsession—horses—and Sara Beth's plan for the rest of winter break. It's cozy and perfect, yet a thrill runs through me once we're done eating and my youngest daughter runs toward the decorated tree to open a present in honor of Christmas Eve.

The three of us join her as she rattles several boxes searching for the best one to unwrap.

"I don't think the one you want is down there, kid," Soren says, shooting a sly grin my way.

Sara Beth plops on the couch and covers a laugh when Rachel glares up at her dad.

"Why not?"

"Because it's so special we decided to keep it hidden in our room," I explain. "Wait here with your dad and sister while I go get it, okay?"

Soren and I discussed whether Rachel was old enough for her own pet, but when Sara Beth promised to help her little sister take care of one, we couldn't pass up the opportunity to give Rachel a bunny for Christmas.

Normally, I'm opposed to pets for Christmas, but when a poor baby bunny was brought into the vet clinic where I work, it seemed like kismet.

Dr. Winston and I worked to get the baby healthy, and now she's ready for our girl. She's even met Sara Beth's old bunny, Whiskers, and the two have been sweet cuddled together.

Snagging the white and brown bunny from her place in the primary room's bath tub, I carefully lower her into a vented and pre-wrapped box.

"Don't worry. You won't be here for long." The bunny shudders, bumping her head against the edge of the box.

I heft the box into my arms and slowly walk back to the living room, making sure to avoid any random toys laying in my path.

Soren has Rachel sitting in his lap on the leather recliner while Sara Beth appears to have picked out the gift she's going to open after Rachel, the small blue and silver wrapping paper shining under the Christmas lights.

Kneeling on the area rug in front of Soren and Rachel, I set the box down with a smile as Rach fights out of her dad's hold to join me, mirroring my position.

"Alright, this is a fragile present, okay? You can't shake it around like you did the others." Rachel gently places her hands on either side of the box lid and solemnly nods. "This is from your dad, me, and Sara Beth because we love you."

"I love you, too. Can I open it now?"

Soren coughs, and I know he's trying not to laugh at her eagerness.

"Wait until I have my camera ready. I want to video this." It only takes a minute, but when I'm finally set up, I press record and mouth, "Go ahead."

Rachel rocks side to side in excitement then, slower than I would have expected, removes the lid. The bunny immediately hops up on two paws, her nose twitching.

"A bunny!" Rachel gasps as the baby startles and skitters back from her loud yell.

"Indoor voice," I caution.

"A bunny!" Rachel tries again, marginally quieter. Her little hands reach into the box and lift the bunny for snuggles against her chest. "Is it a boy or a girl? What's its name?"

"It's a girl, and she's yours, so you get to name her," Soren says.

Rachel bites her lip then glances at Sara Beth. "How'd you name Whiskers?"

"I liked how his nose twitched and made his whiskers tickle my cheek."

"Hmm... They do tickle, but she can't be Whiskers, too." More thinking causes her features to scrunch up. "I'm gonna name her Pipsqueak because she looks like Pipsqueak from the show."

Of course, she went with a *My Little Pony* character.

"That's a cute name, and it fits because she won't get much bigger."

Rachel buries her face in Pipsqueak's soft fur and murmurs, "I love you so, so, *so* much. You're the cutest, softest..."

"Hey, don't insult Whiskers," Sara Beth cuts in.

The two girls bicker over who has the best bunny while Soren grabs my arm and tugs until I'm in his lap.

"Merry Christmas, baby. I'm saving your Christmas Eve present for later," he rumbles.

Cuddling into his heat, I whisper in his ear, "Is it your dick? Because it's been the same thing each year."

"And you love it every time."

"I do." Pressing a kiss to his bearded cheek, I sigh, full of happiness. "I love you."

CHAPTER NINE

DECEMBER 24

BECKETT CALDWELL

My phone rings, and I debate ignoring the call, but Beth leans over to swipe the screen to answer when she sees it's my brother.

Instead of Soren's grumpy face, though, it's my niece and an adorable bunny squished to fit in the small window.

"Look what Mom and Dad and Sara Beth got me! A bunny! His name is Pipsqueak and..." Rachel continues to babble about her new best friend while Beth and I struggle not to laugh at her enthusiasm.

"He's really cute," Beth inserts when the girl stops long enough to take a breath.

Rachel gets even closer to the phone screen, bumping her nose on the camera before whispering, "I know. Don't tell Sara Beth, but he's cuter than Whiskers."

"I heard that!" Her sister calls from the background. Soren and Diana can also be heard chuckling somewhere behind Rachel.

"Well, I can't wait to meet her, kid. Are you bringing her to Christmas dinner tomorrow?" I ask.

She peers back at her parents, and their matching thumbs-up of approval has her pumping her fist in victory. "Yes!" Ducking her head, she starts talking to Pipsqueak. "You're gonna meet Gramps and Grams, Uncle Ezra, Aunt Lauren, Nash, and..."

The list of family members is long now that my siblings are all married with children. Our numbers have grown to football team proportions these days.

"Alright, time to say good-bye to your aunt and uncle." Soren grabs the phone where Rachel has been ignoring it for the past few minutes. Addressing us, he says, "You were last on her list to call with the good news, so maybe now she'll finally start getting ready for bed."

There's a rebellious little grumble that sounds awfully similar to Soren's growls before we promise to see each other tomorrow and end the call.

"I love that girl." Beth sighs, lounging on the sofa with her head propped up on her hand.

"She definitely gives my brother a run for his money. Sara Beth was a handful, but I think Rachel has her beat."

"It's always the babies of the family."

"Except for ours," I point out with a laugh. "Griffen isn't much of a troublemaker and never has been."

"No, I suppose you had that covered," she taunts, "Mr. Bad Boy of Suitor's Crossing."

"I retired that moniker years ago. Besides, you love me, anyway." Kissing her pouty mouth, I groan at the remnants of hot chocolate clinging to her tongue then force myself to retreat.

We've got a Christmas Eve tradition to complete before I'm free to love on my wife for the rest of the night.

"Okay, time for presents. Which one do you want to open first?"

Some of the light dims in her eyes, and I wonder what I said to dampen her mood. Before I can ask, though, Beth uncurls from the couch and grabs a gift set slightly apart from the rest under the Christmas tree.

"This one." She hands it to me, an almost imperceptible tremor in her grip. I'm not sure why she seems nervous. She's been acting strange the past few weeks, but every time I ask if anything is wrong, she brushes me off, saying I'm being paranoid.

I wait until she's seated again then begin ripping the green and gold wrapping paper. Pausing before removing the white cardboard lid on the gift box, I glance up at Beth with a reassuring smile. "You know whatever you got me I'm going to love."

"You're easy to please." The words are a tease, but I can tell she said them on autopilot, her focus on the present in my lap like it's a ticking time bomb.

Curiosity eats at my concern as I toss the lid and lift sparkly red tissue paper to reveal a neatly folded t-shirt.

This is what has her clenching her fists and biting her lip in worry?

The silhouette of a firefighter helmet decorates the center of the chest. An 'EST.' logo with the year is printed inside it. But it's the two words surrounding the artwork that finally settles in my brain and starts a buzzing in my ears.

Fire Dad.

FIRE DAD.

My gaze jerks to Beth, who already has tears threatening to fall down her flushed cheeks.

"Babe, are you..." I swallow the lump in my throat and try again. "Are you pregnant? Are we having a baby?"

"Yes... My doctor's appointment confirmed it. Are you happy?"

"Are you kidding?" I drop the boxed tee and lunge for her, wrapping her in my arms. "I'm fucking ecstatic. We've got a little one on the way, and babies are much better than bunnies."

Beth gives a watery laugh and returns my hug. "They are, aren't they?"

CHAPTER TEN

DECEMBER 25

GRIFFEN CALDWELL

"Damn, Griff, what the hell is that thing?" Beckett hurries to the back of my truck where I'm unloading the family Christmas gift that took months to create. He's been grinning like a fool from the moment he and Beth arrived at Lauren and Ezra's home for dinner.

Always the most lighthearted of our siblings, this over-the-top peppiness is a little much even for him.

"You'll have to wait and see," I say with a grunt as we heft it out of the truck bed and maneuver through the front door of the house.

With my blacksmithing business growing in Guardian Valley, I've had less free time on my hands, but when the idea for a family tree representing the Caldwells came to mind last spring, I couldn't ignore it. Every spare moment has been spent on soldering and hammering the metal into an elaborate tree with winding branches and leaves.

"What is it, Uncle Griffen?" Tristan asks, his jaw dropped wide open, as we cross the threshold.

"It's a surprise. This is a gift for everybody, so we all need to be together to see it," I say.

"I'll get everybody," Tristan volunteers, running from the huge foyer.

Beckett and I continue our trek down the hall to the enormous living room with high ceilings and a wall of windows that looks out on the mountains.

A giant Christmas tree fills part of the space, decorated by family at the bottom, professionally at the top, where Ezra and Lauren couldn't reach. Everything in this place is oversized, but I know my brother wanted to have a home big enough to house all of his siblings and Gramps, along with his and Lauren's children and the rest of his nieces and nephews.

So far, it's doing a good job of providing enough space for everybody to spread out.

A chorus of *oohs* and *ahhs* erupt once Beckett and I enter the living room, deciding to brace the gift against the wall.

"That's some present. Who's it for?" Soren asks.

"It's a family gift"

"Wait, wait," Tristan calls, dragging his mom and Beth into the room. Judging by their aprons, they must have been working on Christmas cookies in the kitchen.

"A gift for everybody?" Curiosity drips from Ezra's tone.

"Yep, so everyone gather around." There's plenty of room. Two sofas and a collection of lounging chairs fill up as everyone takes a seat in anticipation.

A riot of nerves crops up at being the center of attention, but this is my family, so I take a deep breath to relax.

"This idea came to me a few months ago. It was inspired by all the changes we've gone through the past couple of years. It's meant to represent us and our growing numbers." I look pointedly at the children.

"Can I open it?" Rachel asks.

"Why don't you and Tristan both come up here to rip the wrapping paper? But I'll need to finish unwrapping it just to be safe." The kids scream in excitement before rushing forward, tearing at the wrapping paper Heidi and I spent too long taping together.

Once they're down to the cardboard bracketing the iron piece, I wave them back and use my pocket knife to rip the tape open, revealing the massive metal tree.

"Whoa." Sara Beth's is the only reaction as everybody remains silent while studying the piece.

Flushing uncomfortably, unsure if anyone likes it, I gesture to a couple of features.

"It's a literal family tree with the branches, the leaves. They represent each of us, even though I didn't put our names on it. I figured we could showcase it at the lodge as part of our family's legacy. That way we could all see it." I scratch at the back of my neck.

"That sounds like a great idea." Ezra stands and pats my back before pulling me in for a hug. Soren and Beckett follow with Kennedy last.

"This is amazing. I can't believe how talented you are."

"Thanks," I rumble.

There's a sniffle, and we look back to see Beth swiping beneath her eyes. "Sorry, I don't mean to cry. Stupid hormones."

"Hormones?" Kennedy's eyes widen. "Does that mean you're pregnant?"

Beth tenses then nods.

"Oh my gosh!" The women converge on Beth while us guys congratulate Beckett.

"It's about time you've joined our ranks," Wyatt jokes.

"Welcome to the Dads Club."

"You guys are such dorks," Beckett says.

"Oh, and you're gonna be the cool dad?" Kennedy interjects, rolling her eyes playfully.

"Since I'm the cool brother, I think it's natural to assume I'll be the cool dad." Beckett grins.

As everybody devolves into excited chatter about the newest arrival coming to our family, I join Heidi and Joy on the sofa. "You did good, babe," she says, kissing my cheek. "It's beautiful."

"I couldn't have done it without you," I admit. It's because of her that I even considered pursuing blacksmithing. It seemed like a far-off possibility, and then she made it real by being so focused on pursuing her own dreams.

And now we have everything we could ever want. Her photography business, my blacksmithing, and our beautiful little girl.

It's more than I ever thought I deserved. More than I ever thought I'd get.

But thanks to *heart sparks*, they are all mine.

EPILOGUE

DECEMBER 25

GRAMPS

The candles glow on the dining table as the last grandchild is settled in their seat. Glancing around the dark oak, a sense of satisfaction fills my heart. My family is together again.

"You gonna cry, old man?" Greta teases, leaning into me.

"Maybe... I'm not afraid to shed a tear."

"Oh, I know. I remember Game 7 of the World Series when your team lost in that double play during a rally."

"Now that's just cruel. Why would you bring that up on such a joyous evening?"

"Because it's my team that won."

"Rub it in, why don't you?" Shaking my head at her antics, I clear my throat, preparing to say a little something before we dig into the Christmas feast laid out before us.

"Family dinners are important in the Caldwell family. Most of us still get together every Sunday to enjoy time together, but not everybody is always able to make it."

"Everyone has busy lives these days, and that's okay. Life is all about change. About growth. And I'm so proud of each and every one of my grandchildren for what they've accomplished. You've made an old man proud."

"Grandpa..." Kennedy blinks away her tears.

"It's true. Suitor's Crossing is a special place. We know that. *Heart sparks* are always at play. Even if some haven't always believed in their power." I look at a few of my grandsons who used to think that way.

"This Christmas, my entire family is here. From grandkids to great-grandkids. Greta and I couldn't be happier. We love you."

A round of *love yous* travel around the table before I clap my hands with a smile. "Merry Christmas, now, let's eat!"

That's a wrap on our Caldwells! But if you're curious about some of the people mentioned, check out these books next:

Festive Fever (features Thatcher North): Age Gap/Curvy Girl/Christmas Romance

December Desire (features Calder Mayfield): Curvy Girl/Cinderella Vibes/Christmas Romance

Protected by the Mountain Man (features King Bishop): Age Gap/Curvy Girl/Christmas Romance

Pursuing the Mountain Man (features Dr. Winston the vet): Curvy Girl/He Falls First Romance

THANKS FOR READING & DON'T FORGET TO RATE/ REVIEW!

Please consider leaving a rating/review. Ratings & reviews are the #1 way to support an indie author like me.
Also, don't miss out on free books and up-to-date release information. You can sign up for my newsletter here[1].
I appreciate your support!
XO, Hallie

1. https://www.thearrowedheart.com/hallie-bennett

ABOUT THE AUTHOR

Hallie prefers steamy stories where curvy girls are claimed by filthy-talking heroes. And when she ran out of reading material, she decided to write her own stories. If you want a quick, hot read, she's your girl!

www.ingramcontent.com/pod-product-compliance
Lightning Source LLC
Chambersburg PA
CBHW050320200626
46812CB00019BA/2940